THE LITTLE FIRE ENGINE

by Graham Greene

Illustrated by Edward Ardizzone

The Bodley Head – London, Sydney, Toronto

All rights reserved   Text copyright © Graham Greene 1973   Illustrations copyright © Edward Ardizzone 1973   ISBN 0 370 02021 9
Printed in Great Britain for The Bodley Head Ltd, 9 Bow Street, London WC2E 7AL, by William Clowes & Sons Ltd, Beccles
Colour separations by Colourcraftsmen Ltd, Chelmsford   *This edition first published 1973*

Do you remember Little Snoreing where the little train lived?
If you don't you must buy the book about him and read of his
adventures when he ran away into the great world outside.

But there were two characters in Little Snoreing who never

wanted to leave the village they loved so much. They were old Sam Trolley, the fireman, and the Little Fire Engine.

Here is Sam Trolley. He is the father of Joe Trolley, the porter you read about in *The Little Train*.

Years ago Sam had been a sailor. He had known enough of the big world to prefer Little Snoreing. Hurricanes, pirates in the Caribbean, typhoons in the China Sea, desert islands, whales, tornadoes . . . "I'd much rather have my pony," said old Sam Trolley. "My pony, my little fire engine, and my sofa to stretch on at the end of a long day."

Here is the little fire engine. He was built years ago before

motors were invented. Anyway motor fire engines were not
needed at Little Snoreing where if you sneezed outside the
post-office at one end of the village you shook the raspberry

canes in Mrs Brigstock's kitchen garden at the other end. In his time the little fire engine had put out fires in three hayricks, in the chimney of Mr Poslethwaite's cottage (Mr Poslethwaite the sweep not Mr Poslethwaite the engine driver), and he had

helped Sam Trolley to get five little boys' heads out of five railings.

"He's an old salt,"
Sam Trolley would say
with pride, "I'd have
been proud to have him
with me in a storm at sea."

Here is the pony who pulled the little fire engine. His name

is Toby. He was born on Farmer Coote's farm about four miles
outside Little Snoreing on the road to Much Snoreing, the
market town. Sam Trolley was almost as proud of Toby as he

was of the little fire engine. But sometimes he wasn't quite sure—you'll learn why presently.

"Toby," he used to say, "he's a fine pony. I wouldn't ask for a better pony. I've known worse ponies than Toby at sea. But sometimes when I look in his eye, sometimes I think he's ambitious, Toby is," and Sam would sigh and shake his head.

Now I want you to meet
the Mayor of Much Snoreing.
His name is Briggs and he is
a proud, bad man. He wears
a chain round his neck and a
three-cornered hat.
He didn't like Sam

Trolley because Sam refused to salute him when he visited Little Snoreing.

So the Mayor planned a Plan, a really dirty Plan. He wrote to the Lord Mayor of London and said how silly it was for Little Snoreing to have a fire brigade that was only one old man and a horse. "Send us a real motor fire engine to Much Snoreing," he wrote, "and we will put out all the fires in Little Snoreing too."

Old Sam Trolley had a calendar hanging up in the fire station underneath his helmet. There was a red ring round one day— May 30. That was Fire Brigade Day every year in Little Snoreing. For weeks before he had been polishing the brasses and scrubbing Toby till it hurt because on that day he would parade proudly round the streets and collect money for the Firemen's Orphanage. All the children that day were given a holiday, and there would be buns and lemonade and swings and Aunt Sallies on the village Green.

"I'm proud of you both," said Sam Trolley, "and tomorrow all Little Snoreing will be proud of you too." It was quite dark when he went home.

There was a letter on the mat sealed with four red seals and signed Joe Briggs, His Worship the Mayor of Much Snoreing.

Sam Trolley thought of the little fire engine fast asleep and dreaming of tomorrow. He was a man and he couldn't cry, so he blew his nose six times.

"How shall I break the news to the little fire engine and Toby?" thought Sam Trolley. But there was no need. Both of them were woken up by the cries of the children.

"Come and look at the lovely new fire engine."

The Mayor of Much Snoreing was photographed beside the new fire engine with his five new firemen. Somebody joggled the photographer's elbow (I think it was Farmer Coote's little boy Christopher, who loved Toby), so this is how it came out in the newspaper.

All that day Sam Trolley and Toby and the little fire engine stayed at home. In the distance they heard the cheers of the crowd, the brass band, the popping of ginger beer bottles in the Vicarage garden. They had never been left out before. On the next page you will see what they missed.

Poor old Sam Trolley couldn't even smile when he saw the paper. The rent for his cottage would soon be due and he didn't know how to pay it. He had nothing in the world but his uniform and his little fire engine and Toby (but he didn't trust Toby). "How am I going to earn my living?" wondered old Sam Trolley.

The little fire engine wondered: how can I help Sam? If only I could turn myself into a boat, thought the little fire engine, we would sail away to sea together, but whoever heard of a boat with wheels?

Toby thought: I love Sam and I love the little fire engine, but a horse must look after himself in this world; he whinnied and kicked his stall because he was bored. I might be a circus horse, he thought, and jump through hoops. . . .

Sam Trolley thought and thought and smoked and smoked.

I might become a policeman, he thought, but what would become of the little fire engine? I might become a shopkeeper but what would become of Toby? Suddenly he had an idea.

"I'll be a higgler," said old Sam Trolley. "But not a higgler
like old Jim Bottle."

All through the summer, up hill and down dale, Sam Trolley
and the little fire engine travelled the roads. They saw the wild

roses come out in the hedges and the roads became dusty with flower dust which is called pollen. Toby suffered from hay fever and sneezed a good deal.

One could see them from a long way off because of the clouds of dust Toby kicked up with his hoofs. Sometimes the little fire engine felt a little sad because it reminded him of smoke. But summer doesn't last for ever. Autumn comes and the leaves fall.

It would be dark when they started out, dark when they came home. After the autumn, icy winds blew and winter was here.

Winter in the old days meant warm fires—fires to sit by and sometimes fires to put out. Now it meant mud and rain for old Sam Trolley, the little fire engine and Toby.

Old Sam Trolley suffered badly from rheumatism.

The little fire engine suffered badly from rust.

Toby suffered from boredom.

When the alarm clock rang by old Sam Trolley's bed at six o'clock on a cold winter's morning he thought it was a fire alarm and dreamed of a great fire. "Hi-yi-yi-yi!" he cried, (which is the fireman's call) and felt for his axe.

But outside there was no fire—only snow, falling over the roofs and the roads, covering the fields and the farms.

Up hill and down dale trudged the little fire engine. Old Sam Trolley looked like a snowman, and the little fire engine like a

big Christmas pudding. "It will be a sad Christmas for we three," thought Sam Trolley.

Just then he heard a bell clanging and down the hill came tearing the new fire engine, gleaming with brass work.

"A snowman, a snowman," shrieked the five new firemen with yells of mocking laughter, and they pelted Sam with snowballs as they rushed by. One snowball hit Toby in the eye. "This is the end," thought Toby. He hated to be laughed at.

All the children went to Much Snoreing to a party at the new fire station, but Sam Trolley and the little fire engine tried to do their best. It wasn't much of a tree and you can't make a higgler's van as smart and shining as a fire engine, and Toby didn't even pretend it was much fun.

That night when
everyone was asleep
Toby kicked a hole in
his stable door and
stole away.

What a morning for poor Sam Trolley. "Were we unkind to
him?" Sam Trolley wondered. "I never thought Toby would
desert us. There is nobody left to pull the higgler's van. We are
ruined," he said to the little fire engine. "I have no money to
pay the rent."

It was early morning when Toby trotted back to the farm
where he had been born. Nobody was about but a cock and
four silly hens.

Sam stayed shut up in his cottage all through Christmas because he was afraid of the rent man. He had a plum pudding and a dozen mince pies, and he rationed them as though he were on a desert island. He had half a mince pie every morning for breakfast, half for lunch with a slice of pudding, he left out tea, and at supper he sometimes had half a mince pie and sometimes a slice of plum pudding. "The great thing," Sam said, "is variety."

New Year's Eve came and there was only one mince pie left.

That night when all
the new fire brigade
were dancing or
drinking at the Town
Hall, Much Snoreing,

a terrible fire broke out in
Farmer Coote's stables.

Toby had been fast asleep in
his stall when the smoke blew

in under the door, dreaming of Sam and the little fire engine, and that they were all at a fire together. He woke and a real fire was there, but he was all alone, except for the other horses and they were too frightened to know what to do. They neighed

and tossed and screamed. "Keep your heads," Toby cried, but they paid no heed.

"You cowards," Toby cried, "listen to me. I'm a fire horse. I know. All together at the stable door, CHARGE," but only a white foal listened to him and charged too. The door bent and bent, the lock creaked, the door burst open . . .

Meanwhile at the firemen's ball Captain Whiskers and Lieutenant Stout . . .

Old Sam Trolley dreamed of roast pork with plenty of crackling which tasted oddly like mince pies. Suddenly from

outside came a long whinny. It
was Toby's warning whinny,
the whinny he always made
whenever there was a . . .
"FIRE," cried Sam Trolley,
leaping out of bed. Then he
thought, "I'm dreaming again.
Toby's run away." He looked
out of the window and there was
Toby.

Back through the night galloped Toby with the little fire
engine bounding at his heels. "Hi-yi-yi," cried old Sam Trolley,
ringing his bell for all he was worth.

It was New Year's night and the sky was full of stars, but
none of them twinkled as brightly as the little fire engine's
brasswork.

Farmer Coote heard the beat of hoofs coming down the road. "We are saved," he cried. "It's the little fire engine back on the road again."

People talked about that night for the rest of their lives, and how they laughed the next morning.

I don't really need to tell you any more. You can imagine it all for yourselves. The new motor fire engine and the five firemen were all sent back to London in disgrace.

Sam Trolley got a medal and here it is.

The Mayor got a bowler hat (that meant he had stopped being Mayor).

Toby got a pound of sugar.

And the little fire engine got a grand new fire station to live in happily ever after.